MATTHEW, MARK, LUKE AND JOHN

MATTHEW, MARK,

PEARL S. BUCK

Illustrated by Mamoru Funai

LUKE AND JOHN

WCP

**Pearl S. Buck
Writing Center Press**

Perkasie, Pennsylvania

This reprint edition has been published in honor of the 125th birthday celebration of the author Pearl S. Buck on June 26, 2017. This edition is the work of three editors from the Pearl S. Buck Volunteer Association's Writing Center Press: Linda K. Donaldson, Anne K. Kaler, and Cynthia L. Louden.

ISBN-13: 979-85509-81733

Pearl S. Buck Writing Center Press
Green Hills Farm, 520 Dublin Road
Perkasie, Pennsylvania

www.pearlsbuck.org/writing center

Matthew, Mark, Luke and John was originally published by
The John Day Company, New York in 1967.
Book text ©1966, Pearl S. Buck Foundation, Inc.
Mamoru Funai illustrations ©1967, The John Day Company, Inc.

Books and Stories for Children by Pearl S. Buck

The Beech Tree, 1954 (later published as *The Heart's Beginnings*)
The Big Fight, 1965 (later published as *Tiger Boy*)
The Big Wave, 1948
The Chinese Children Next Door, 1942
The Chinese Story Teller, 1971
Christmas Day in the Morning, 1955
The Christmas Ghost, 1960
Christmas Miniature, 1956
The Dragon Fish, 1944
A Gift for the Children, 1940 (collection of stories)
        The Clouds
        The Dark
        Five Children
        The Moon
        Peter and the Squirrel
        The Rainbow
        The Snow
        The Star
        The Sun
        Thunder
        Tracks in the Snow
        What the Children Do in Summer
        What Happens in Spring
        When Fun Begins
The Heart's Beginnings, 1955 (previously published as *The Beech Tree*)
Johnny Jack and His Beginnings, 1954 (alternate title: *The Secret of Everything*)
The Little Fox in the Middle, 1966
Little Red, 1945
The Man Who Changed China: The Story of Sun Yat-sen, 1953
Matthew, Mark, Luke and John, 1967
Mrs. Starling's Problem, 1973
My Several Worlds, (abridged for younger readers), 1957
One Bright Day, 1950 (previously published as *One Happy Day*)
One Happy Day, 1947 (later published as *One Bright Day*)
The Secret of Everything, 1954 (alternate title: *Johnny Jack and His Beginnings*)
Tiger Boy, 1965 (previously published as *The Big Fight*)
The Water-Buffalo Children, 1943
The Young Revolutionist, 1932
Yu Lan: Flying Boy of China, 1945

List compiled thanks to Marie Toner,

Curator Pearl S. Buck International House and Museum.

He woke early. The rumble of trucks and cars, the trotting of donkey's feet, the slow thud of a horse's hooves, sounded on the bridge above his head. It was the beginning of another day.

"My name is Matthew," he said.

He spoke the words aloud and slowly, so that he would not forget them. They were the only English words he knew because he was in Korea. Here he had been born, his father an American soldier, and here he had lived for all the eleven years of his life. He lived alone now under a bridge in the city of Pusan.

When he had lost his Korean mother, nearly a year ago, he had taken shelter under the bridge in a rainstorm. He could not understand how he had lost her. Or had she lost him? They were very poor, he remembered. They lived in a small earthen house in a village with her parents. He knew they were her parents for she called them "Father and Mother," but

what he could not understand was that he was never allowed to call them "Grandfather" and "Grandmother," even though his cousins did so. For that matter, he was not allowed to say "Cousin" to his cousins, nor Uncle and Aunt to his mother's brother and sister. Only his mother could be called by name.

"Why can I not call the others by name?" he had asked his mother.

"Because your father was an American," she had replied. "Therefore you belong to him, not to us. Children in Korea belong to the father. His name was Matthew, and I gave you his name."

He had been much surprised to hear that his father was American.

"What is American?" he had asked his mother.

"It means someone from America," his mother had replied. "Someone different from us. You look like him. Your eyes are too light, your hair is too red. Here in Korea you see we have black eyes and hair."

"Do you mind?" he had asked.

He had watched her face to see if she minded. Sometimes other children teased him and called him "American" or "Foreigner," or even "Round-eyes." She had only pursed her lips. Then she smiled,

"How would you like to go to the city tomorrow?" she had asked. "I will buy you a new jacket."

He forgot his first question in another. "But do you have money?"

It was seldom she had money but she put her hand into her inner pocket. "I have saved enough from my sewing."

It was the next day that he remembered to ask the next question. In the excitement of buying the new jacket, he had thought of nothing else. His old jacket had been too small for a long time, but he had no other. When he put on the new one in the shop it was too big and he felt lost in its looseness, but his mother had insisted upon it.

"It must last you for a very long time," she said. "I may never be able to buy you another," she added.

For some reason he did not understand, tears came into her eyes and she wiped them away with the edge of her wide sleeve.

He had been frightened. "I am not going to die, am I?" he had asked.

She had tried to laugh, but the tears kept rolling out of her eyes as fast as she wiped them away.

"Button your new jacket," she said, trying to stop crying. When he had buttoned it, she looked at him strangely.

"I wish your father could see you," she said.

11

It was now he thought of the next question.

"Where is my father?"

She had shaken her head. "He went away to America."

The shopkeeper had been listening. Now he spoke.

"Ah, he is one of Those!"

She had counted out the money and they left the shop. The street was crowded and he walked behind her as usual. For some reason she never let him walk beside her. Since he had learned to walk this was her rule and he obeyed. Suddenly she stopped and turned to him.

"Stay here," she told him. "I paid the shopkeeper

three pennies too much. I must go back and get those pennies. Here – hold my purse."

She thrust the small bag of coins into his hand and hurried back to the shop and he waited for her. It was a long time and he grew tired of standing. He sat down on the edge of the curb, tucking up his jacket to keep it from the dust. Again he waited and still she did not come. He knew it was a long time for the sun had been pouring straight down into the street when she left him and now it had slipped behind the houses. The shadows were chill and he was glad he had his new jacket. Besides, he was hungry.

He had searched every face that passed and none was his mother's face. At last he rose to his feet. It occurred to him that he should go to the shop and see if she were there. He thought he knew the way, but when he tried to remember where the turns were, he was soon lost. He never found the shop, although he had often tried to do so, and never again had he seen his mother's face.

The first night he had crept under the bridge and cried himself to sleep. Now of course he knew better than to cry. He had made himself a sort of home there, and he came back to it every night. Still when he woke in the morning, as he did now, he always had a moment of two of feeling lost again. He was quite alone, and sometimes he wished that he had a friend, a boy like himself. There were such boys, he knew, for more than once someone would stare at him and mutter –

"Another one of Those!"

The cave under the bridge was big enough, too, for another boy, maybe even two or three. It was a big bridge, made of stone blocks in three arches over a river. It was lucky that the river had changed its course in the centuries since it had been built and what had been a torrent was now a brook. It was convenient to have water so near in which to bathe himself and wash his undershirt, but in winter it froze. He had learned how to make a fire in the back of the cave and to melt ice in a tin can he had found in a garbage pail outside the American camp. He knew now what an American was, for some times an American soldier gave him a coin for polishing his shoes, or just for begging, after the money his mother had given him was gone.

He tried not to think about his mother. Had she wanted to find him as he wanted to find her? For days, for months, he had searched the passing faces. He had given up at last and he had only this pain in his breast if he let himself think of her.

He got up now and lit a little fire between two stones. Over these stones was a piece of wire fencing he had twisted off the bottom of the barricade around the American camp. Spread across the stones it made a place for his can of food to be heated. This morning he had rice left over from yesterday and some kimchee he had bought. It was a windy autumn morning and the smoke blew out from under the bridge. He heard footsteps and in a moment someone appeared at the nearest arch of the bridge. It was the policeman.

"You, redhead," the policeman called. "What have I told you about making a big fire? Do you want me to lose my job? People will think the bridge is burning."

"A stone bridge?" Matthew laughed.

"Stone or not, one is forbidden to build fires under bridges," the policeman replied.

"It is the big wind, not the big fire," Matthew said.

But he covered the fire with some ash. The policeman was kind and let him live under the bridge. Sometimes he even brought him a small bag of rice or a round bun of bread stuffed with meat. Today he tossed the boy a coin.

17

"Buy yourself some socks," he said. "Winter is coming."

Winter! Matthew dreaded the winter. In spite of the fire, he could never get warm. He thought of this as he ate his rice and kimchee now. Perhaps if he could earn a little more money he could go to the pawnshop and buy an old quilt to spread on top of his straw bed. It had not been easy to get even the straw. People bought it to burn in their kitchens, and he did not dare to enter a doorway to steal. Instead he begged handfuls of straw from the bundles farmers brought into the city to sell. Sometimes they gave it to him but sometimes they refused and cuffed his ears.

"Foreign brat!" they bawled at him.

Why was he foreign? He thought about this as he washed his tin can after breakfast. The river water was already cold. When he splashed it on his face his skin felt cold as the wind dried it. He did not wash very often in the winter. It was always his dream to earn enough money to buy a hot bath in the bath house. Yet he was not sure he would be allowed to enter there, since they called him foreign.

It was a bright day, he discovered, when he came out from under the bridge. The sun never reached his cave and he never knew until he left it what the weather was. Now the day was heartening. Already the sun was warm. He climbed up the steep bank of the riverbed to the street above. It was busy with morning life. Shops were open, people were coming and going, cars moving. He turned into a side street. It was the season for ripe persimmons and when he passed a pile beside someone's doorway he longed to pick up a few except that it might be stealing. But was it stealing when they were everywhere? One never knew whether people would be kind. Sometimes they were kind and would even give him a persimmon. More often they set the dogs on him.

And as he walked, he considered what he could do to earn some money to buy his quilt. His luck was always at the camp. There, though he was never allowed inside the gate, the guard shouting at him if he tried to sneak through, the American men coming and going sometimes gave him money or a foreign magazine or some cigarettes, either of which he could sell.

There was a big tree near the gate whose roots, rising out of the earth, made a comfortable niche where he could sit while he waited. It was still early when he got there and he prepared himself to wait in patience.

He had no sooner settled himself, however, than a strange thing happened. A woman came running out of the gate, sobbing as she ran. She was young and a Korean. He knew the difference by her dress. She wore a full dark red skirt and a white Korean silk bodice. He saw this because she stumbled and sank down on the ground, her long black hair in its braid falling over her shoulder into the dust.

"Aie, aie," she sobbed.

"Why are you crying?"

He called out the question from the road, and she lifted her head and stared at him, her eyes wide and wet with tears, "Another one of Them –" she sobbed, and getting to her feet, she ran on until she was lost in the crowd.

This was puzzling enough, but in a few moments an American in uniform came out of the gate leading a small boy by the hand. He was not a very small boy, perhaps six or seven years old, and he was neatly dressed in short dark trousers and a red sweater. He did not look Korean but neither did he look American as the man did.

The American looked left and right and down the street. "Where did your mother go?" he asked in Korean.

It was not very good Korean, but Matthew could understand it. The boy shook his head. Matthew answered for him, of course in Korean since he spoke no English except his name. He pointed to the distance.

"She run that way."

The man looked at him. "What's your name, boy?" he asked.

"My name is Matthew."

The man looked, unbelieving. "Matthew? For a Korean boy?"

"I am also American," Matthew said.

The man gave a great sigh. "Then here is your brother. His name had better be Mark. Matthew, Mark, Luke and John, God bless the beds that you lie on —"

His face twisted as though in sudden pain. He felt in his pocket, brought out a fistful of money and stuffed it into Mark's pocket. Then he turned and marched into the gate and closed it. The two boys stood looking at each other. What Matthew saw was a sturdy boy

with a round face, rosy cheeks, bright brown eyes, and short golden brown hair. He was not at all thin and he looked very clean, as though he had just come from a bath, and his clothes were new. Even his shoes were new, brown leather over white socks.

"Is your name Mark?" Matthew asked.

The boy looked at him as though he did not understand.

"Mark?" Matthew repeated.

The boy smiled. He had a nice cheerful smile, and his name must be Mark, Matthew decided, since he did not deny it. Matthew took two steps forward. Now he was face to face with Mark.

"Where do you live?" he asked.

Mark looked at him, not answering. He was still smiling, but now uncertainly. Suddenly, Matthew understood. Mark could not speak Korean! Then, of course, he did not know what Matthew was saying, for he, Matthew, could not speak English. What could they do? For a moment, he thought he would go on his way. Indeed, he even began to walk down the street. As soon as he did so, however, Mark ran after him and clung to his hand. He looked at Matthew and tears came into his eyes. He poured out English words, trying not to cry.

"I don't know what you're saying," Matthew replied. "But you had better come with me."

He took Mark's hand and led him toward the bridge. Suddenly he thought of the money Mark had in his pocket. Now that there were two of them, they really must buy a quilt, a big one that would cover two boys instead of one. He stopped at a pawnshop and hand in hand they went in. An old man in a patched white robe stood behind the counter.

"What do you want?" he asked.

"A quilt, big enough for two," Matthew replied. "And it must be thick and warm."

"You are very small to be buying your own quilt," the old man said.

"We are orphans," Matthew said.

The old man picked up a pair of iron-rimmed spectacles from the counter, put them on and stared at the boys.

"Ah, you are two of Those," he said.

"Yes," Matthew replied.

"Are you brothers'?" the old man asked.

Matthew hesitated. Then he answered out of his heart.

"Yes, at least we are going to be. I just found him today."

The old man shook his head. "I don't understand that but never mind. The important question, have you money?"

Matthew turned to Mark. "Give me the money," he said.

He pointed to Mark's pocket and now, of course, Mark understood. He took out the handful of bills and gave them to Matthew.

"How much is a quilt?" Matthew asked.

The old man waited before he answered. His eyes were greedy at the sight of so much money but he was still good enough to remember that these were two lonely children.

"First choose the quilt," he said. "Then let us talk of the price."

He brought out three quilts, very slowly, for he was quite old, and laid them on the counter.

"Nice quilts," he said, "and all cheap."

Matthew felt each of them. The one in the middle was the thickest and it was covered with gray cotton cloth patched in only a few places.

"We will take this," he said. "How much is it?"

The old man struggled with himself. It would be pleasant to ask a big price and take all the money. Yet would he have an easy heart if he did so?

"Where do you live?" he asked.

"Under a bridge," Matthew said.

"A bridge?" the old man repeated. "Only beggars live under bridges. Are you beggars?"

"Sometimes, if I can't find work to do," Matthew said.

"You are very small to work," the old man replied.

"I can work," Matthew said bravely. "And now there is no one else to take care of my brother."

The old man sighed and gave up the idea of asking too much money.

"It is a good quilt," he said. "I could sell it for a great deal of money, now that winter is near. But since you are orphans – I will give it to you for one-third the price."

"Thank you," Matthew said.

He paid for it, took the quilt in his arms, and Mark held the edge of his coat instead of his hand.

The old man felt sorry for them. "Poor children," he said. "Where is your father?"

"He is gone away to America," Matthew replied. He spoke only of his own father, because he did not know about Mark's father, but perhaps one was enough.

"Does he send you money?" the old man asked.

"No," Matthew said.

"Then where did you get this money?" the old man asked.

"Another American gave it to us," Matthew answered.

The old man gazed at him over his spectacles.

"I don't understand," he said.

"Neither do we," Matthew said, "but thank you for asking so little for the quilt."

So saying, he left the shop, Mark clinging fast to his coat, and together they went to the bridge. He showed Mark how to climb down the bank and creep under the first arch and climb again until they reached the cave hidden behind a wall of rock. Above their heads were the street and the noise of passing vehicles and feet. Inside the cave the light was dim, but everything Matthew had was there, his wooden box with a few clothes, the box he had begged from a shopkeeper, some pictures he had torn out of an old magazine, his chopsticks and the round tin cans he used for food bowls and the old tin teakettle he had found on a trash heap. It had leaked but he paid a wandering tinsmith a little money to mend it and now it was as good as ever. He spread the quilt over his heap of straw and then sat admiring it. Really the cave looked nice, he thought, now that they had the quilt. And there was still some money left. He counted it and taking out only a little for food, he put the rest in his secret hold, behind a loose stone.

All this time, while he had been busy, Mark was sitting on a ledge watching him and saying nothing because he could not speak Korean. Now Matthew sat on the ledge, too, to think what to do. How could he live with someone with whom he could not talk? He wished so much to ask Mark who he really was, why he was able to have such good clothes, who the woman was who ran away sobbing, why he could not speak Korean, how he happened to be in a camp. Not one question could he ask. He would simply have to teach Mark how to speak in Korean. Well, then he had better begin. His eyes fell on Mark's neat brown leather shoes. He pointed to them.

"Shoes," he said in Korean.

"Shoes," Mark repeated in Korean.

Thus was begun their new life together. Slowly, slowly, a day at a time, word after word, Mark learned to speak Korean. And word after word, too, Matthew learned English. For, it occurred to him one day, would it not be a wonderful good thing to know the language of his American father in case, just in case, some day they discovered each other, by chance of course? But had he not discovered Mark by chance? In a very few weeks, he wondered how he had ever lived without Mark.

I must have been very lonely without knowing it, he thought.

Indeed he had been lonely, for Korean boys teased him on the streets and he had learned to avoid them, preferring loneliness to their shouts and laughter, because, they said, he looked so strange. Now he had Mark and they were never separated. By day they begged or worked when they could find work, such as sweeping the street in front of a shop. Begging was easier now that there were two of them, especially begging from Americans, who gave them money and sometimes bread and other foods. Sometimes, too, they did not like the foods, but they ate them anyway, for food is food. At first they thought chewing gum was food. They chewed for a long time and when it seemed to do no good, they swallowed the gum until one day an American soldier boy had laughed a big laugh and told Mark it was not to be eaten.

"Then why chew it?" Matthew asked Mark.

Mark put the question to the soldier boy who took off his cap, scratched his head and could not answer.

It was not long before Mark learned to speak Korean easily and though English was harder, Matthew learned, and after a few months, the two boys had no trouble in talk.

By now, too, it was winter. Snow fell and the wind blew in from the cold gray sea or down from the mountains behind the city. Mark felt the cold more than Matthew, who had already lived through a winter under the bridge. They slept warmly enough together under the quilt but in the day they had to get food somehow. There were times when Mark cried because he was so cold. His hands were swollen with frostbite and Matthew kept watch of his cheeks and nose to see that they were not bitten with frost. He decided that something must be done. He must find boards and strips of tin or heavy paper and build some sort of shelter. But where could he find such materials without stealing them? To steal he was afraid, for his mother had taught him not to steal.

At last he decided to talk with the policeman. Now and again the policeman crept under the bridge to see how the boys fared. Sometimes he said they should go to an orphanage, but Matthew begged him to leave them where they were.

"Soon I shall be grown up," he told the policeman, "and then they will just send me away. Orphanages are for small children, not me."

"This second one looks very small," the policeman argued. "See him shivering with cold!"

"I take care of him," Matthew said proudly. "We need a few boards and something to keep the wind from the cracks between. Then we will be warm."

The policeman went away grumbling, but after the next snowstorm he came back.

"They're taking down some old huts to put up a new building," he told Matthew. "It is near my beat and you may carry away some boards. It is not my affair if a few boards are taken."

So in the night, Matthew and Mark carried boards and the policeman gave them a handful of nails and Matthew used a round stone for a hammer. He put up a wall of boards and he found old paper on the streets and filled the cracks, and the wind no longer circled the cave under the bridge. In the winter nights the two boys talked together as they lay under the quilt and Matthew learned Mark's story.

"We lived in Seoul," he told Matthew, "and my father in America sent us money. He sent enough for food and clothes and we lived in a nice room. Then suddenly he stopped sending money. My mother wrote him, and he wrote back to tell her he was married now to an American wife. Another American man came to see my mother, but my mother would not talk to him. At first she would not talk, but when we had no more money, she did talk to him. The man put me out of the room so he could talk to my mother at night. I sat on the street waiting for them to stop talking. She cried, but we had no money except from this man. One day he went away, too. She heard that he had been sent to the camp in Pusan and so we came here. All our money was gone when we reached the camp. But the man was not at the camp. Some other man, an officer, was rough to my mother. He told her to get out. So she ran to the gate because she was afraid, and I could not run so fast. I fell down and another man helped me and took me to the gate. But she was gone. He was the one who named me Mark. Who was Mark?"

"I don't know any Mark except you," Matthew said. "And who is Luke and who is John?"

"I don't know them," Mark said.

He was sleepy now and he fell asleep, curled against Matthew, to keep warm. But Matthew laid awake for awhile, thinking about himself and about Mark.

Other people were all born into families, it seemed, and only they were born alone, without a family to care for them. How did it happen that they were born? Why was it that their fathers came from far away, strange men who were different from Korean men? And why could their Korean mothers not keep them? And why, oh why, did other boys laugh at him and Mark and tease them as though they were homeless dogs? He asked himself such questions but he could not answer one of them and so at last he fell asleep.

Somehow the winter passed. Snow ceased to fall, the wind blew less bitter, and along the roads outside the city small, green weeds straggled toward the light. Matthew and Mark were hungry for green vegetables and they joined other poor people to dig the weeds to cook and eat with rice or millet. How pleasant was the warmth of the sun! At noon it was so warm that they threw off their ragged jackets and let the sun shine on their bare backs. The birds, silent through the winter, came back with the spring, and sang their songs again. The mountains, shedding their winter snows, lifted their gray heads against the blue sky.

All might have been almost happy for Matthew and Mark except that one evening when they came back to the city, their basket heaped with dandelion, shepherd's purse, young clover and such sweet fresh greens, their friend, the policeman, was waiting for them at the bridge. He was not alone. With one hand he grasped the torn collar of a boy. One might have thought he was frightened, this boy, except for his eyes. They were large, round and blue.

"Here is another one of Those, like you," the policeman said. "I have just caught him. He was stealing the money out of a beggar's bowl – that old beggar who sits always at the temple gate yonder. He had fallen asleep for a few minutes and this boy was emptying his begging bowl."

"I don't know this boy," Matthew said.

"I never saw him before," Mark said.

The boy looked from one face to the other, his bright eyes darting here and there, but he said nothing. He had a round naughty face, his brown hair was dusty, and he was very dirty.

But he did not look hungry or thin.

"I ought to put him in jail," the policeman said.

"Don't put him in jail, please," Matthew said. "I can see that he is one of us. He can live in our cave. There is room for one more."

The policeman shook the boy by the collar but not too hard. He made his face stern but since he was quite a young man still, he could not look too stern.

"What will you do if he steals again? He is a thicf and a clever one. See how fat he is! You are both thin but he – he is a bad one."

"We will give him some of our food," Matthew said. "Look at our basket – it is spring now and

we can dig greens. And we can all work. He will work, too. People want to make gardens and plant seeds. We can do such things."

The policeman put on an angry face. "What will you do if he won't work?"

"Let us try," Matthew said.

He took the boy's hand. "Will you try?" he asked.

The boy nodded.

"Well, for a while," the policeman agreed. He let go the boy's collar. "If he were only a year older, I would put him in jail."

"How old are you?" Mark asked the boy.

"I don't know," the boy said.

"Seven? Eight?" Matthew asked. The boy was only up to his shoulder, but then during the winter he, Matthew, had grown tall and very thin.

"If you say seven, I am seven," the boy said. "If you say eight, I am eight."

He had a saucy voice and the policeman pretended to slap him.

"You will have trouble with this one," he said, "and when you do, then call me. I can still put him in jail."

"Here – take this."

He gave Matthew a piece of money and went away. The three boys looked at each other.

"What is your name?" Matthew asked the new boy.

"I have no name," the boy said.

"What do people call you?" Matthew asked.

"They don't call me. I have no people," the boy said.

"No mother?" Mark asked.

"I've forgotten," the boy said.

"Where do you live?" Mark asked.

"Nowhere," the boy said.

"But at night?" Matthew urged.

"In a doorway – sometimes in the railroad station but they chase me out."

"Come into the cave," Matthew said.

They crept under the bridge and into the cave.

"This is nice," the boy said, looking around.

During the winter, Matthew and Mark had indeed tried to make the cave more comfortable. They had found some old boxes for seats and they had found a board for a table.

"It is better than nothing," Matthew said proudly, "and you can sleep under our quilt with us. It is big enough for three. And your name will be Luke."

"What is Luke?" the boy asked.

"It is a name," Matthew said, "an American name. I can see your father was an American like ours. We are Those. That is what people call us here – Those."

Now began a new life in the cave because of Luke. Before he came, Matthew and Mark had lived together without quarreling, Mark always obedient because Matthew was taller and older. But Luke obeyed no one. He had lived by stealing instead of working and he did not like to work. When Matthew found a job for the three of them in a fruit shop, putting the fruit away at night and setting it out in the morning and then sweeping the floor, Luke did not do his share of the work. Instead he played about, talking and laughing and pretending to work. The second day, Matthew saw him put out his hand quickly and steal an orange and hide it in his pocket.

"Luke!" he shouted.

Luke was startled and people turned their heads to see why there was a shout. Matthew did not know what to do. If he made Luke put the orange back everyone would know Luke was a thief and the policeman would put him in jail. He said nothing until they got back to the cave and then he talked to Luke.

"You must not steal," he told Luke. "I am ashamed that you steal. If you steal you will be put in jail. Where is the orange? I will take it back."

"I ate it," Luke said. "And why shouldn't I steal? That old man will never miss an orange. I like oranges."

"I will buy you an orange if you will promise me not to steal any more fruit," Matthew said.

"Why should we waste our money?" Luke said. They were sitting around their box table eating their supper. He ate more than the others and he kept on eating very fast. "Besides," he said, his mouth full of rice and cabbage, "Mark ate part of the orange."

Matthew turned to Mark. "Did you?"

"Yes," Mark said in a small voice. "Luke told me to eat some."

"Didn't you know it was wrong?"

Matthew's voice was so stern that tears came into Mark's eyes and rolled down his cheeks.

"You didn't tell me before," he said in a whisper.

"But I thought you knew, by yourself," Matthew said. "Did we ever steal anything before Luke came?"

Mark could not speak. He shook his head.

That night Matthew could not sleep. He turned and tossed because he did not know what to do. Luke was not sorry. He thought it was clever to steal. Mark was gentle and younger than Luke. Matthew decided to go and see the friendly policeman.

It was near midnight when he crept out from under the quilt. He left the two boys sleeping and he came from under the bridge and went down the street and around the corner to where the policeman was on duty.

"There you are," the policeman said when he saw Matthew in the light of the streetlamps. "Why are you out so late?"

"I am looking for you." Matthew said, and he told him his trouble.

The policeman leaned against the wall and listened. "I was afraid of this," he said. "Luke has been alone in the world since he was little and he is used to stealing to live. His father – no one knows where the father is. Luke doesn't remember him."

"Where is his mother?" Matthew asked.

"His mother is a thief, too, and she is in jail. They used to steal together."

"Doesn't he have a grandfather or an uncle or some-one?" Matthew asked.

"They don't want him," the policeman said. "He is one of Those. Let me put him in jail."

"No," Matthew said.

"You'd all be better off in an orphanage," the policeman said.

"No," Matthew said again.

"Why won't you go into an orphanage?" the policeman asked. "They will feed you and clothe you."

"It is more like a family as we are," Matthew said.

"Then you are responsible for Luke," the policeman said. "As though you were his father."

"I will be responsible for him as though I were his father," Matthew said.

He walked alone through the quiet moonlit streets and back to the cave again. The boys were sleeping but he could not sleep. What would he do if Luke would not change? Would he be able to watch Luke all the time? And would Luke make Mark into a thief? These questions Matthew asked himself over and over again but he could not answer them. He could only do his best every day, but it would not be easy.

It was not easy. For a few days Luke was good. He even tried to help in sweeping out the fruit shop. Matthew began to hope that Luke would not steal anything again. Then it happened. It was night. They were getting ready for bed. Luke pulled off his jacket and under it, Matthew saw a new cotton shirt. His own had long since worn out.

"Where did you get that shirt?" he asked.

"A man gave it to me," Luke said.

Matthew looked straight into Luke's eyes. "Luke, is that true?"

"I have one, too," Mark said. He pulled open his jacket. "Luke gave it to me."

"Where did you get the shirts, Luke?" Matthew asked.

Luke tried to laugh. "Don't act so big, Matthew," he said. "You are not really our father."

"Take that shirt off," Matthew said. "Take yours off, Mark. Now Luke, tell me where you got those shirts."

For a moment he wondered if he would have to fight Luke and tear off the shirt. He gazed straight into Luke's eyes and Luke stared back at him. For a moment he stared, trying to be bold, and then his eyes fell. He peeled off the shirt slowly.

"I did it for Mark," he muttered.

"You did it for yourself," Matthew said. "And you hurt Mark because you are teaching him to steal. I cannot allow you to do this. I am responsible for you."

"What means responsible?" Mark asked.

"It means that if Luke steals, the policeman will blame me, Matthew said.

Luke looked surprised. "But you don't steal."

"No," Matthew said. "Of course I don't steal. I would be ashamed to steal."

Luke looked puzzled.

"Do you understand?" Matthew asked.

"No," Luke said.

Matthew sighed. "We had better go to sleep," he said. "Tomorrow I will get up early. I will take back the shirts."

The next day he did take back the shirts. He explained everything to the shopkeeper.

"Keep the shirts," the shopkeeper said. "I cannot sell them now because they have been worn. But you are an honest boy."

"I will pay for them as soon as I can save the money," Matthew said.

Time passed. The summer came and went. It was autumn again. The leaves fell, persimmons ripened and lay in golden piles under the trees, in courtyards and streets. Luke had been almost good all summer. Once he had stolen a piece of soap from a woman who was washing clothes in the river but she screamed and he gave it back. Once he took a small cake from a baker's tray and ate it quickly but Matthew saw it and paid the baker. Persimmons were different. There were so many of them everywhere, they were sweet with juice and Luke liked them too much. Again and again he ran off and came back with yellow stains about his mouth.

Matthew was angry and sad at the same time. Worst of all, Mark came back one day with yellow stains.

"Mark, did you steal?" Matthew demanded.

"Luke gave me some persimmons," Mark said. His round face was so innocent that Matthew said no more. Persimmons were plenty and perhaps he should not be too angry. But he was still not happy and he went back to the policeman.

"Is taking persimmons stealing?" he asked.

"It's very near," the policeman said. "Is it that boy again? Once a thief, always a thief!"

Matthew went away quickly then. Persimmon time would soon be over. Then he must watch Luke very carefully as winter came on. Life was always harder in winter. Snow fell, winds blew, and work was scarce.

On top of everything else, they found John. It was a rainy afternoon and they were out looking for food. Sometimes rich people threw quite good food away in garbage pails. Then dogs and poor people would snatch it for themselves. Since it was raining heavily, not many people, even poor ones, would be out and there would be few dogs.

"Let's go to that Choi family house," Luke said. "Sometimes they throw away bones with meat still left on them."

To the Choi house they went. No one was at the back gate when they arrived. No one? There was a very small boy there, hiding behind a crooked pine tree. He was eating a rotten pear. As soon as Matthew saw him, he recognized him. He was one of Those. He had brown skin but his eyes were gray and his hair was not black.

"Who are you?" Matthew asked.

The little boy was frightened. He could not have been more than five years old. He dropped the pear.

"I don't know," he said.

"What is your name?" Mark asked.

"I have no name," the boy said.

"Where do you live?" Luke asked.

"Nowhere," the child replied.

"And your mother, where is she?" Matthew asked.

"Mother? What is that?" the little boy asked in reply.

"Oh, let him come with us," Mark cried.

Matthew hesitated. Yet another? But in the end, of course, the little boy did go back with them to the cave. And since they had found the skeleton of a chicken and some pork ribs with meat left on them, they had food.

"What shall we call our new brother?" Mark asked.

"We will call him John," Matthew said.

But in his heart, he felt frightened. Three children, younger than he, all looking to him for food and clothes and shelter – it was hard to be responsible for so many, especially for Luke. It was difficult to be a father. He began to understand why sometimes fathers went away, and left their children. Well, he would never go away, nor leave these three who trusted him and had no one else.

The next day was especially cold. The sky was gray. The air was still and great flakes of show began to fall. The three boys had no money for food and there was no work to be had.

"Let's go by the American camp," Mark suggested. "Remember the man at the gate gave us some money?"

"We are not beggars," Matthew said.

"No, we are only hungry," Mark replied.

There was nothing else to do and so they went to the gate of the American camp. To their surprise, many children were going in.

"Let's go with them," Mark said eagerly.

Matthew hesitated. These children were all warmly dressed and they looked well fed.

"We don't belong with them," he said.

Just then the same American who had given them money came to the gate.

"Hurry up, kids," he said. "Santa Claus is waiting. Lots of goodies for everybody!"

He pushed the children along and without recognizing them he pushed the four boys along with the others. In a moment they found themselves in a big room. It was warm and the air was fragrant with pine

branches on the walls. In the middle of the room was a tall pine tree covered with small bright lights and ornaments. Beside the tree was an old man in a red suit. He had a long white beard.

"Santa Claus, Santa Claus," the American kept saying.

He pushed the children toward the old man, and as each passed, the old man gave the child a package.

To Matthew, Mark, Luke and John he gave packages, too. In each was a pair of warm socks, a pair of warm gloves, some candy and an apple. The boys could not believe what they saw. For besides these gifts there was food – cakes and nuts, rice and meat and hardboiled eggs, and each could eat as much as he wished. Even Matthew forgot himself and ate until he could eat no more. The room was so warm that he was too hot and sweat streamed down his face.

The kind American saw his distress.

"Take off your jacket," he suggested.

Matthew shook his head. "I cannot," he said.

"Why not?" the American asked.

Matthew was ashamed to reply. He could not tell the truth. He could only shake his head again.

"Come on," the American urged. "Don't be shy. I'm your friend. My name is Sam."

Still Matthew was ashamed. At last, seeing that Sam was waiting, he unbuttoned his jacket and showed him. He had nothing on underneath.

"I see," Sam said kindly. "It's jacket or nothing. Well, here is something to cool you off – a nice, big dish of ice cream."

He handed the dish to Matthew. On it was a mound of white snow. At least Matthew thought it was snow for he had never seen ice cream. He tasted it. It was not snow. It was sweet and delicious. Sam stood watching and smiling.

"Good?" he asked.

"Good," Matthew said.

Everyone was eating ice cream now. It was at this moment, however, that Matthew saw Luke. Luke had eaten his dish of ice cream very quickly. Just as quickly, he now took another dish from the table, and he began emptying the ice cream into the pocket of his jacket.

"Luke!" Matthew shouted. "Don't steal!"

Everyone looked at Luke. Matthew was very angry

He went to Luke and put his hand into the pocket to take out the ice cream. He could not. It had melted. He drew out his hand. It was sticky. Sam laughed, and all the men laughed.

"Here," Sam said. "Wipe your hand on this paper napkin."

He gave the paper to Matthew. "What's the matter?" he asked Matthew.

For suddenly Matthew was trying not to cry. He had not cried since he was very small and had lost his mother. He had not cried because he knew there was no one to listen. Now he felt helpless. Luke was stealing again. It was too much to bear. All his life suddenly seemed too much for him. He remembered everything at once, the loneliness, the cold winters, the search for work and food, these three boys for whom he was responsible. How could he be responsible for them when Luke was still a thief?"

"I'm not really their father," he sobbed.

"Come here with me," Sam said.

He led Matthew aside into a small room.

"Now tell me what's wrong," he said.

He sat down and drew Matthew onto his lap. "Tell me everything," he said.

So Matthew tried to stop crying so that he could tell Sam everything. He could not stop at once, and while he sobbed, he felt Sam's arms warm about him. It was the first time he had ever felt arms about him. He stopped crying and looked into Sam's kind blue eyes. Sam was saying something.

"How would you like to be my son?" he was asking.

Matthew could not understand, not at first.

"Are you my father?" he asked.

"No," Sam said, "but I would like to be."

"How can you be my father if you are not?" Matthew asked.

"I could adopt you as my son," Sam said, "and you could adopt me as your father."

Matthew thought about it.

"I would like to have a father," he said at last.

"But would you like to have me?" Sam asked.

Matthew looked at Sam for a minute. He saw a kind face, honest eyes and a firm mouth. It was an

American face. He was half American himself, and he liked this face.

"Yes," he said. "I would like you to be my father."

Then he remembered. "What about Mark, Luke

and John? I can't leave them. They wouldn't know what to do without me. I'm their father. They haven't any other."

Sam smiled. "You're much too young to be a

father. They really need someone older. Look here –
we'll put them in our company Child Care Center here.
They'll have warm clothes, plenty of food, and they
can go to school"

Matthew was still troubled. "Luke will not want to
go to school."

"Yes, he will," Sam said. "When he finds that he
doesn't need to steal because he has food three times
a day and he has his own clothes and things, he'll
change. We'll see to that."

Every story has its end, and this is the end of
Matthew's story, except it is also a beginning. It was
the end of living under a bridge, the end of being cold
in winter, the end of being hungry. It was the beginning of being the son of Sam and his wife Ruth.

Of course, Matthew could not know all at once
what the new life would mean, a life with a real father
and a mother, a life in a new country where people
would be glad he was American, even if he was only
half, and where they would not mind that he was also
half Korean. Indeed, they would find that interesting.

He began to understand something about the new
life, however, the very day of the Christmas party.

For after the party the four boys did not go back to the cave under the bridge. They stayed in the Center and each of them had a bed to himself and some warm clothes and his own bowl and chopsticks and all the rice and vegetables he could eat and sometimes even a little meat or an egg.

This was change enough, but for Matthew there was a greater change. He began to understand, after a few days, that Sam was more than a kind man. He really wanted to be a father. He came one morning and explained something to Matthew.

"You see, Matt, you're my son now. Of course we'll have to wait for papers to be signed, so people will know I'm your father, and Ruth – that's my wife in America – is your mother."

"Does she want to be my mother?" Matthew asked. He had forgotten what it was like to have a mother.

"Oh, indeed she does," Sam said. "I called her on the telephone all the way across the ocean yesterday and I wish you could have heard her happy voice. She said you were the best Christmas gift she could ever have. And she wants you to come quickly."

All this and much more Sam told to Matthew. He came every evening to the Center and he showed pictures to Matthew, pictures of his new mother, who had a smile on her pretty face, and pictures of his new home that he would soon see.

"That's the window of your room," Sam said, pointing to a window upstairs. "And here's the big maple tree. We'll put a swing on this branch. And we have three apple trees in the backyard."

They talked so often of his new house that Matthew began to feel that nothing would be strange to him when he got there, and he was impatient to begin living his new life in America. All except for one thing – he could not forget Mark, Luke and John. They seemed to be very happy here in the Center with the other boys, and at first they could not believe he was going to America. America? Where was it? Why did he want to go there when now he had plenty to eat and warm clothes to wear? These were good arguments but he wanted more. He wanted to be somebody's son. He wanted to have a father and a mother of his own. He tried to explain this to the three boys but they could not understand.

"Maybe this new father and mother will run away too," Mark said.

"Sam is not a running-away kind of father," Matthew said, hoping that this was true.

Nevertheless, because of what Mark had said, he was all the more ready to begin his new life. One day, Sam came in very cheerful.

"All right, Son," he said. "The last paper is signed and delivered and just in time. We're going home, you and I. Come along."

"But I'm not packed," Matthew exclaimed.

"Leave your old clothes here," Sam said. "You and I are going out this morning to buy you new things – just enough to get you home. Your mother will want to buy the rest. We leave at noon, so hustle!"

Hustle they did, and they barely had time to buy the new suit and hurry back to the Center to say good-bye to Mark, Luke and John. They were in such a hurry that no one had time to feel sad. The three boys could not realize that Matthew was leaving them, nor could he realize it, either. For now he knew that he really

was Sam's son. He had wanted to know it before but he did not quite dare, not until he knew he was going to America. Suddenly he also realized he was in a taxi-cab on the way to the airport, leaving the three boys behind. He grew very silent, so silent that Sam spoke.

"What are you thinking about, Son?"

"I'm thinking about Mark, Luke and John," Matthew said.

He was thinking of how the three boys had looked when he left them at the Center. He had stepped into the cab and glancing back he saw the three standing in front of the other boys. They had all come crowding around when they heard Matthew had a real American father who was taking him to America. Everyone was excited and shouting good-bye and good luck, except Mark, Luke and John. They were not shouting. They were standing close together, holding hands tightly, as though they were afraid they might lose each other.

"They didn't want me to leave them," Matthew said, now in the taxicab.

"Look at me," Sam commanded.

Matthew obeyed. He looked into Sam's kind blue eyes.

"I want to hear you say 'Father,'" Sam said. "Dad later, maybe, but now call me your father."

It was true that Matthew had never spoken these words. Why? Because he had not been sure that Sam really would not run away as the other fathers had done. Now he was sure.

"You are my father," he said, his voice firm.

Sam could not speak. He just put his arm around Matthew's shoulders.

Yes, this was the beginning of Matthew's life as the son of Sam and his wife Ruth. He did not forget Mark, Luke and John, but he did not know what to do about them except to remember them. The jet plane carried him across the Pacific Ocean and across the Rocky Mountain, across plains and rivers until it reached the big airport in the city of New York.

"Your mother will be waiting for us," Sam told him.

He was right. They came out of the jet, they walked through the corridors of a huge building until they saw a waiting crowd. In front of everyone, Matthew saw her.

"You'll know her when you see her," Sam had told him. "She's not tall, not short. She's not fat, not thin.

She has brown hair and brown eyes, and it's likely she'll be wearing a red suit of some sort."

"There she is!" Matthew cried.

"Ruth!" Sam shouted.

She came running toward them and Sam caught her in his arms. For one short minute Matthew felt shy, but only for one minute. Then she put her arms about him, too.

"O Matthew," she said, "how happy I am that you're our son!"

She was really happy, he could see that. Her eyes were bright and her cheeks were pink.

They found a cab and they put their luggage into it with them and went to a railroad station. There they took a train, still together. All the way, Matthew felt happy. He did not talk because his father and mother talked all the time, and he wanted to listen. Every now and again they looked at him and smiled and he smiled back. After an hour or so, the train stopped and they got out, with all their luggage, and there was a car waiting. It was their car, Matthew discovered, and this made him proud. It had not occurred to him that he would belong to a family that had a car of its own. He was so busy finding out what the buttons and handles were for that he forgot to be quiet and listen. Instead he asked questions.

"What's this? What's this for?"

They were at the house before he expected, and there it was, just as his father had said it would be, a white house with green shutters, a tall maple tree and a big yard. They got out of the car and went inside. He saw a pleasant living room with books along a wall, and stairs. They went up the stairs, and his mother opened a door.

"This is your room, Matthew," she said.

He went in and looked around. It was a nice room with white curtains at the windows, a bed, a desk, and chairs and shelves to put things on. There were already some books on the shelves.

"All for me by myself?" he asked.

"For you by yourself," his father said.

"Thank you," he said. Then he remembered. "Thank you both, Father and Mother."

"We are happy to have you," his father said.

"Oh, very happy," his mother said.

So Matthew came home at last. It was home and yet it was new. There was much for him to discover. He had never lived in a house before, not a house that was also a home. He went up and down stairs many times, just to see what it was like, because he had not lived in a house with stairs. There were all sorts of machines he had never seen before, machines to wash with, to clean with, to look at, to listen to, and he had to learn how to work everything. He learned how to play baseball for his father taught him, and then boys came over to play, boys who lived in the other houses along the street. He went to school every day and met other children. School was difficult at first because he had never been to school, and he had to begin at the beginning with the smaller children but he worked hard so that he could catch up with the boys his own age.

Time went fast with so much to learn and soon it was Christmas again. It was his first real Christmas and it was very exciting. He had never heard the Christmas story, and his father and mother had to explain it to him. They explained, too, how Christmas happiness overflows into giving gifts.

"Since we cannot give gifts to the Christ Child as the three Wise men did on that first Christmas, we give gifts to those we love," his father said.

Matthew planned gifts for his father and mother and each helped him with his gift for the other. Then he had some special friends at school, and for them he made gifts, and his father helped him. And all the time while he did these things he kept thinking about Mark, Luke and John far away across the sea, and how they had stood holding hands together when he left them. He had never forgotten them – not for a single day. Busy and happy as he had been, he thought of them and was often troubled. Had they run away, perhaps, and were they trying to live alone under the bridge? This thought troubled him so much that finally his father, seeing his face sad one night, had asked him what was the matter. Matthew told him.

"Oh, that we can soon find out about," his father had said. "I'll write a letter."

He did write a letter and back had come the answer that Mark, Luke and John had not run away. They were still in the Center and now they were going to school. Soon a letter from them came to Matthew. The writing was in English. It was crooked and the letter was a very short one, but it told him that the three boys missed him. He answered it and so letters began to come and go across the sea.

"I want to send them a Christmas present," Matthew told his father when Christmas was near.

"Why not?" his father replied.

So Matthew and his father and mother bought new clothes and a toy for each boy and sent them off in time for Christmas.

It was on Christmas morning, however, that Matthew put into words something that he had been thinking about for a long time. He had not spoken of it, for he felt it might seem ungrateful when he had been given so much to want something more. The gifts this Christmas morning were generous and each was what he wanted – a small camera, a new sweater, a baseball bat of his own and a ball, books – oh, many things.

"Get everything you want, son?" his father asked.

Matthew nodded. "Thank you," he added.

But something in his eyes showed through, and his father saw it.

"Come now," he said. "Tell me what else you want.

"It is not wanting exactly something," Matthew said. His English was good but he had his own way of talking. "It is something I am still remembering."

"What is it?" his father asked.

"I am remembering last Christmas," Matthew said. "I am remembering Mark, Luke and John, and how I am their only father."

"Oh, come now," his father said. "It's very well to think of them but I still insist that you are too young to be their father."

"I must be their father until they find new fathers," Matthew said.

He forgot his gifts, thinking of last Christmas and how all the change in his life had come about. Really it had happened because Luke had stolen the ice cream and put it into his pocket. Had Luke stopped stealing? And were they happy, those children to whom he had promised to be a father?

"Well, then," his father was saying. "I daresay we'll be able to find some new fathers for them. Eh, Ruth?"

His mother was looking at Matthew, her eyes tender with sudden tears.

"I am sure we can find some fathers for them," she said, "and mothers to go with the fathers. Fathers alone are not quite enough."

"Hear that, Matt?" his father said. "You can't be father and mother, too, and they'll need both."

It was a thought. Matthew looked from one loving face to the other.

"What shall we do?" he asked.

"Let's sit down and consider," his father said.

They sat down on the floor at the foot of the lighted Christmas tree and they considered.

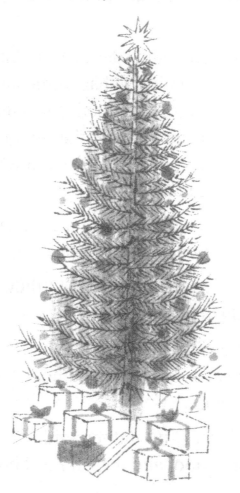

"On this street," his mother began, "there are many fathers and mothers. If we told them about Mark, Luke and John –"

His father interrupted.

"There'd be more than enough to go around. Of course there will be some fathers and mothers who won't want to go through all that paper work I had to go through for you, Matt."

"There'll certainly be three couples who will think it was all worthwhile, just as we do," his mother said.

This was the way it was on that Christmas day. Once they had decided, his father and mother began making telephone calls.

"Come to our house this evening, will you?" they said to the neighbors. "We have something exciting to tell you about –"

Something exciting it certainly was. People came into the house that evening, and while the Christmas tree was bright with many lights, Matthew told them about Mark, Luke and John. He told them everything, how at first he had lived alone under the bridge and how one after the other he had found Mark, Luke and John.

"That was how I became their father," he said at last. "And now I would like to find new fathers for them, because I can't be a mother, too, and each boy needs two people, father and mother."

The people listened, smiling, even laughing when they heard how Luke had put ice cream into his pocket, but at the end they were not laughing. Some of them were wiping tears from their eyes.

"How about it, neighbors?" Sam asked.

That was how it began, but it was not finished in a day, nor even in a few days.

"We didn't expect that though, did we, Son?" Sam said. "Remember how long you had to wait for me to get all the papers signed and finished? And you waited, didn't you? Well, Mark, Luke and John must wait, too. But just remember that it wasn't only you who waited. I waited and so did your mother and we were impatient, I can tell you, but we had to wait. So while Mark, Luke and John wait over there, just remember their new fathers and mothers are waiting here."

"Will Mark, Luke and John be here before next Christmas?" Matthew asked, that night before he went to bed.

"Oh surely," his father said.

"Oh yes," his mother said, "long, long before next Christmas."

"Then that will be the happiest Christmas of all," Matthew said.

It was the end of the day, a happy Christmas day. Suddenly he was sleepy. So much had happened and he did not need to worry anymore about Mark, Luke and John. He was not their father now, just their friend.

"Good night, dear Father and Mother," he said, "and thank you."

He let them kiss him for once, although he was really too big for kissing, he thought, but they were good to him and his heart overflowed. He went upstairs and suddenly he had a new feeling. All this time he had been too shy to sing even the Christmas carols, but now to his surprise, he wanted to sing. He opened his mouth and his voice came out loud and clear.

"Joy to the world," he sang.

. . . Downstairs two people, hearing that young gay voice, looked at each other and smiled as only a man and woman can smile at each other when they share a child.

"He's *singing*," Ruth whispered.

"Thank God!" Sam said.

About Child Sponsorship

"Our treasure is in our children, for in them is our future.
And what a future!" - *The Joy of Children*

The legacy of Pearl S. Buck unites nations, societies, communities and individuals with an appreciation for cultural differences and a commitment to service.

Pearl S. Buck International, along with generous donors, caring child sponsors, Champions for Children, individual members and Corporate Partners, upholds that mission.

Children are waiting for someone like you to become their child sponsor and make a real difference in their lives. We are happy to match you with a child in greatest need.

"If our American way of life fails the child, it fails us all."

For more details about Child Sponsorship contact:
Pearl S. Buck International
520 Dublin Road, Perkasie, PA 18944
Phone: 215-249-0100
Fax: 215-249-9657

Pearl S. Buck International is ranked as one of the Top 5 most
fiscally efficient child sponsorship organizations in the United States.

About the Author

Pearl S. Buck, born in Hillsboro, West Virginia, the child of missionaries to China, left a legacy as the first woman to receive both the Pulitzer and Nobel Prizes for Literature. Pearl S. Buck International continues her humanitarian mission toward world equality.

Beloved for giving America its first view of Asia in her novel, *The Good Earth*, Pearl Buck spent the first 40 years of her life in China and the remaining 40 years living at Green Hills Farm in Bucks County, Pennsylvania.

Ms. Buck's prolific writings span many genres – autobiography, biography, fiction and non-fiction. In addition to nearly 100 novels, she wrote hundreds of articles, essays, poems, short stories, plays, screenplays and speeches centered on themes of racial discrimination, social class or cultural inequality, and treatment of the world's children.

In 1949, along with other prominent Bucks County citizens, Ms. Buck began the Welcome House Adoption program, which spent 65 years finding forever homes for more than 7,000 children. With the adoption program no longer in place, services now concentrate on helping children within their native countries by providing educational, health and social services for them.

In the United States, Pearl S. Buck International serves our community by providing resources toward cultural programs that raise awareness, increase understanding and celebrate cultural heritage. Pearl S. Buck's efforts toward elevating the humanity of all people became one of the cornerstones for today's diversity and inclusion programs.

Today, Pearl S. Buck International preserves her National Historic Landmark Home and Museum as a working community of historic, cultural and artistic programs and events to further her original humanitarian goals. The board of directors, administration, staff and volunteers are commited to carrying forward Pearl S. Buck's legacy into tomorrow's world.

About the Illustrator

Mamoru Funai is a native of Wahiawa, Kauai, Hawaii. As a youth, Funai attended Eleele Elementary School and Waimea High School. He furthered his education at the Honolulu Academy of Arts, the Art Institute of Pittsburgh, the Cleveland Institute of Art, and the William Patterson College of NJ, leading to a Bachelor of Arts degree and a Master of Arts degree.

For nearly twenty years, Funai worked as a professional illustrator for the American Greeting Corporation. He also worked as a free-lance illustrator in New York and New Jersey. It was through his contacts with The John Day Company in New York that Mamoru was hired to illustrate both *Matthew, Mark, Luke and John* as well as another of Pearl S. Buck's children's books, *The Big Fight*.

An author himself, Funai in 1972 wrote and illustrated *Moke and Poki in the Rain Forest*, the adventures of two *menehunes*, said to be a people who live in the deep rain forests and hidden valleys of the Hawaiian Islands, far from the eyes of normal humans. In December 2016 Funai's latest book *The Monkey Pod Tree*, a collection of stories told by a Japanese-American boy growing up in the small village of Wahiawa, was published and is available online.

Mamoru Funai has graciously and generously gifted his illustrator's rights to this reprint of *Matthew, Mark, Luke and John* to the Pearl S. Buck Volunteer Association's Writing Center Press and Pearl S. Buck International.

The Monkey Pod Tree

No one knows for sure, but the Monkey Pod tree in Wahiawa, Kauai, must be 100 years old by now. It grows in front of the Buddhist Temple, spreading its branches over the playground where children once laughed and played. Villagers consider that tree a landmark, and if it could talk, it surely would tell stories of life in Wahiawa. Of course, trees can't talk, yet some stories are meant to be shared.

Sunday, December 7, 1941…As a native of Wahiawa, Kauai, Hawaii, Mamoru Funai remembers that date perfectly. Pearl Harbor began the little known story of Japanese-American families living in Hawaii and the affect that attack had on their lives.

That memory inspired *The Monkey Pod Tree*, a collection of short stories of a boy growing up in a small Hawaiian village before and during World War II. Mr. Funai's personal experiences and enduring friendships authenticate his stories of boyhood innocence, personal challenges of war, and the heritage of the Japanese-Americans.

The Monkey Pod Tree tells about the simple pleasures of the past, the meaning of family traditions, and the ties that bind friendships. Historical events change island life forever; however, the people of Wahiawa call on their courage to remain strong, while they continue to hope for a better life.

The
Monkey
Pod
Tree
By Mamoru Funai

About the Publishers

WCP

Pearl S. Buck Writing Center Press

"Writing at a Writer's House"

The legacy of Pearl S. Buck unites nations, societies, communities, and individuals with an appreciation for cultural differences and a commitment to service. As volunteers at her Pearl S. Buck National Historic Landmark House, we strive to preserve and promote Ms. Buck's extraordinary legacy through public tours and community programs.

The Writing Center offers ongoing educational writing programs – conferences, workshops, classes, guest speakers, monthly Writers Guild meetings and discussions on the works of Pearl S. Buck. Our Writers Guild consists of volunteers – working in the spirit of Pearl S. Buck and Richard J. Walsh, her editor, publisher, and second husband – to enable, encourage, and nurture ideas for writers developing their craft.

Our biannual Pearl S. Buck Online Literary Journal – featuring fiction, poetry, essay, and memoir contributions from our program participants – can be found at our blog site **www.psbwritingcenter.org**. To help our writers self-publish books, we launched the Pearl S. Buck Writing Center Press (WCP) in 2016.

Check the **www.psbi.org/writingcenter** for a list of our classes and program offerings. For more information, please email us at *clouden@pearlsbuck.org*.

"In a mood of faith and hope my work goes on…

I am a writer and I take up my pen to write."

- Pearl S. Buck